THE
GRUFFALO'S
CHILD

Julia Donaldson
pictures by Axel Scheffler

Dial Books for Young Readers New York

The Gruffalo said that no gruffalo should
ever set foot in the deep dark wood.
"Why not? Why not?"
"Because if you do, the Big Bad Mouse will be after you.
I met him once," said the Gruffalo.
"I met him a long, long time ago."

"What does he look like? Tell me, Dad.
Is he terribly big and terribly bad?"

"I can't quite remember," the Gruffalo said.
Then he thought for a minute and scratched his head.

"The Big Bad Mouse is terribly strong,
and his scaly tail is terribly long.

His eyes are like pools of terrible fire,
and his terrible whiskers are tougher than wire."

One snowy night while the Gruffalo snored,
the Gruffalo's child was feeling bored.

The Gruffalo's child was feeling brave,
so she tiptoed out of the gruffalo cave.
The snow fell fast and the wind blew wild.
Into the wood went the Gruffalo's child.

Aha! Oho! A trail in the snow!

Whose is this trail and where does it go?

A tail poked out of a log-pile house.

Could this be the tail of the Big Bad Mouse?

Out slid the creature. His eyes were small.
And he didn't have whiskers—no, none at all.

"*You're* not the Mouse."
"Not I," said the snake.
"He's down by the lake—eating gruffalo cake."

The snow fell fast and the wind blew wild.

"I'm not scared," said the Gruffalo's child.

Aha! Oho! Marks in the snow!

Whose are these claw marks? Where do they go?

Two eyes gleamed out of a treetop house.

Could these be the eyes of the Big Bad Mouse?

Down flew the creature. His tail was short.
And he didn't have whiskers of any sort.

"*You're* not the Mouse."
"Too-whoo, not I.
But he's somewhere nearby, eating gruffalo pie."

The snow fell fast and the wind blew wild.
"I'm not scared," said the Gruffalo's child.

Aha! Oho! A track in the snow!

Whose is this track and where does it go?

Whiskers at last! And an underground house!

(Could this be the home of the Big Bad Mouse?)

Out slunk the creature. His eyes weren't fiery.
His tail wasn't scaly. His whiskers weren't wiry.

"*You're* not the Mouse."
"Oh no, not me.
He's under a tree—drinking gruffalo tea."

"It's all a trick!" said the Gruffalo's child
as she sat on a stump where the snow lay piled.
"I don't *believe* in the Big Bad Mouse . . .

"But here comes a little one, out of his house!
Not big, not bad, but a mouse at least—
you'll taste good as a midnight feast."

"Wait!" said the mouse. "Before you eat,
there's a friend of mine that you ought to meet.
If you'll let me hop onto a hazel twig,
I'll beckon my friend so bad and big."

The Gruffalo's child unclenched her fist.

"The Big Bad Mouse—so he *does* exist!"

The mouse hopped into the hazel tree.

He beckoned and said, "Just wait and see."

Out came the moon. It was bright and round.
A terrible shadow fell onto the ground.

Who is this creature so big, bad, and strong?
His tail and his whiskers are terribly long.
His ears are enormous, and over his shoulder
he carries a nut as big as a boulder!

"The Big Bad Mouse!" yelled the Gruffalo's child.
The mouse jumped down from the twig and smiled.

Aha! Oho! Prints in the snow.

Whose are these footprints? Where do they go?

The footprints led to the gruffalo cave,

where the Gruffalo's child was a bit less brave.

The Gruffalo's child was a bit less bored . . .

and the gruffalos snored
and snored and snored.

For Franzeska —J.D.
For Freya and Cora —A.S.

First published in the United States 2005
by Dial Books for Young Readers
A division of Penguin Young Readers Group
345 Hudson Street
New York, New York 10014
Published in Great Britain 2004
by Macmillan Children's Books
Text copyright © 2004 by Julia Donaldson
Pictures copyright © 2004 by Axel Scheffler
Printed in Belgium

1 3 5 7 9 10 8 6 4 2

Library of Congress Cataloging-in-Publication Data
Donaldson, Julia.
The Gruffalo's child / Julia Donaldson ; pictures by Axel Scheffler.
p.   cm.
Summary: The Gruffalo's child goes out to find the
Big Bad Mouse she has heard so much about.
ISBN 0-8037-3009-8
[1. Animals—Fiction. 2. Curiosity—Fiction. 3. Mice—Fiction.
4. Stories in rhyme.] I. Scheffler, Axel, ill. II. Title.
PZ8.3.D7235Gs 2005   [E]—dc22
2004008671

The art was created using pencil, ink,
watercolors, colored pencils, and crayons.